Jealous of Josie

by Barbara M. Linde • illustrated by Helen Poole

"This is Josie," Miss Laurie said.
"She is joining our class."

"Hi, Josie!" we all said.

"Josie, would you like to be the line leader?" asked Miss Laurie.

"I wanted to be the line leader," I whispered.

"Josie, can you help me pass out the paper?" asked Miss Laurie.

"It's *my* turn to be helper today,"
I said to Olivia.

"Which puzzle do you want?" asked Miss Laurie.

"I like the one with the dogs," said Josie.

"That's the one *I* was going to do!" I said.

"Emma, you've done this puzzle many times," said Miss Laurie. "Let Josie do it today."

"Fine," I said. "Who cares?"

"I think you're feeling a little jealous of Josie," Miss Laurie said.

"But Josie gets to do everything," I said.

"It's her first day," said Miss Laurie.
"Can you be in charge of showing her
around the playground?"

14

"Hey, Josie," I said. "Do you want to play?"

At recess, Josie and I
did everything—together.